Bully and Crush

Eloise Scar

Contents

Chapter 1 - Aiden

He punched me in the side and I fell to the ground with a loud crash. I yelped and others who were watching laughed. The boy on the left kicked in the shin and legs. I was sure that was going to bruise. The boy on the left kicked me in the arm and shoulders while the other boys attacked my back.

It was horrible but I've gotten used to the pain. I've been attacked several times over the last week and lately it's been getting worse. I would usually just pass out from the exhaustion or faint. Either one works, I'd be unconscious to know what was happening, I'd rather not know what was happening to me.

After a couple more minutes of kicking the boys were starting to get tired and slowed their rhythm down. They sighed in exhaustion and backed away.

I slowly maneuvered out of my huddle and stretched my limbs. I scanned my body, nothing was broken but some parts were badly bruised. I tried to stand up but my leg was in bad shape. I fell straight back down and gasped in pain. I made a second attempt to stand up and succeeded. I straightened up my clothes and dusted my pants.

I limped towards my locker and shoved some books into it. I closed it and headed towards my next class. I was already used to the beatings everyday but sometimes I think it's a little much, don't they ever get bored of hitting me?

I walked past the office to my class. I shuffled into the class and scurried to the back of the room. I grabbed the seat farthest away that didn't have another student in it. No one ever sat next to me, well except for my best friend, Louis. People believed that if they talked to me or interacted with me that they would get bullied too. Louis was an exception. Louis, my best friend, was the brother of my worst nightmare, the bully.

I barely went to Louis's house because I'd have to see his brother. But when I did go, Louis would make sure that I wasn't going to get hurt. Louis would beat up his brother for me. My hero. I snickerd slightly at my remark. The teacher walks in and begins class. Guess, no ones sitting next to me again.

Ms Benard began talking about chemical reactions and some other chemistry stuff that I didn't care about. Let's face it, who even likes school? I didn't.

I finished class and headed to my next class. I carefully avoided Aiden, the schools bully. Unfortunatly, my next class was gym. I didn't hate gym, I just didn't like it. Aiden is in my gym class. So is Louis, so that made everything better. It kind of canceled out each other. I can't get bullied becuase Aidens brother was here.

I quickly ran into the changing room and slipped off my shirt and pants. I threw on a white teeshirt and some basketball shorts.

Today, we were running relay races. Running was fun because it was something that I was good at. I could block out the world for a couple of seconds and just focus on running.

The group of kids walked outside to the track that was around the corner. "Alright everybody! It's racing time!" My gym teacher yelled. "Everybody look at the sheet of paper to find out who your partner is." The teacher pointed to a sheet on the bench. I quickly scanned the sheet to see who was my partner. I was crossing my fingers hoping and begging that I wouldn't have Aiden has my partner. I guess my luck ran out because as I apporached my name, I saw that my partner was the one and only Aiden.

Chapter 2 - The bet

I groaned. I meant to do it in my head but it accidentally went out of my mouth. I rubbed my forehead and sighed. Guess today was gonna be horrible. Louis can't even save me now.

I stared at Louis to get his attention but he didn't give me the time of day. He was to busy talking to his partner. I could hear footsteps behind me and the hairs on the back of my neck stiffened.

"Hey partner." I turned around to see Aiden standing there. Even though I basically hated his guts he was a good looking guy. I'm not gay but even straight guys can tell if another's hot.

Aiden was wearing black basketball shorts and a over sized tank top. He had messy hair and hazel eyes. I realized I was staring too long.

"H-Hi." I squeaked. Aiden patted me on the back real hard.

"We're gonna have fun together aren't we." He winked at me. Why did Aiden wink at me? Maybe his eye was itchy. Whatever, doesn't concern me. All I did was nod my head up and down

. I dragged my feet over to the starting line. We were racing against another group. I put my foot on the white line an leaned in position. Aiden did the same thing. In a matter of seconds I heard somebody count down then a gun shot.

I started to run. I picked up the pace and was halfway done when Aiden passed me like it was nothing. Only a couple seconds behind and I crossed the finish line. Aidens group of friends came and congratulated him for getting first place.

Louis congratulated me for getting second with a pat on the back. Aiden and I won the first race. Now it was time for the second one. We both got into our positions and once we heard the shot we sprinted off to victory again. Our last match was against our partners. Oh how wonderful, I get to lose against Aiden.

Aiden came up to me and put his arm on my shoulder wrapping it around me. I could feel the hot breath on my neck. He leaned next to my ear. "Wanna make a bet?" He whispered.

I froze. What type of bet? What will I have to do? What if I loose? What will happen?

"Oh stop worrying ya weirdo." He complained. "It's a simple bet. I win, you do what I want, you win, I do what you want." He smiled. That's the first time he smiled at me in my whole life.

We got into starting positions and I was about to worry. I don't want to loose, Aiden will probally make me his personal slave or something like that for the rest of my life.

Once I heard the shot I dashed off as quickly as possible trying to beat Aiden. I started off strong, Aiden was right behind me. I looked backwards and watched him slightly. He made everything seem like effortless. I could hear his heavy breathing, I'm sure he could hear my deathly breathing. In a matter of seconds Aiden caught up right next to me and we were running together. I could see the finish line.

Aiden kept slightly running into me. He did the unthinkable. While he was running inches away from me he slapped my butt. Hard. I squealed and tumbled over. Aiden laughed and ran ahead into the finish line that was right in front of us. Typically bully, always trying to cause me to get hurt. He crossed the white line and claimed first place. I, on the other hand, am on the ground. My legs all cut up and bleeding.

The pain was terrible but not as bad like when I get beatings. I tried to lift myself up but couldn't. Help was running towards me. I could see Louis with a worried face, along with others. I'm surprised I could even get that much attention.

The gym teacher came over and crouched down towards me. "You alright, kid?" He asked. I could only nod my head. I felt a little lightheaded. "Hey! Someone get this kid to the infirmary!" The teacher yelled towards the kids. The closest person next to me just happened to be Aiden.

Aiden picked me up, putting his hands through my legs. Why was he carrying me princess style. I groaned out loud and tried to wiggle out of his grasp. "Shut up and put your arms around my neck." Aiden snapped. I put my hands on his shoulders. They were so broad and musclier. Aiden frowned. "Ethan, I said my neck." I groaned once more and followed his orders. I placed my arms around his neck and locked my fingers.

Aiden kept walking. I felt even dizzier so I put my head on his shoulders. This was probably a bad move but I couldn't keep my head up anymore. We were almost to the nurses office when I passed out. Wow, did I seriously pass out in Aidens arms? I mentally hit myself on the forehead.

When I woke up I was on a white bed, there was a curtain around me and a mysterious body sitting next to me with it's head on the bed. I attempted to sit up and fix my messy clothes but because of the person I couldn't move much. I tugged the person on the shoulder slightly. It groaned. More like, he groaned. I tugged slightly harder. "Stopp.." he grumbled.

I knew who it was. "Aiden, get off me." I hissed. I pushed him harder and he flung off the bed and onto the ground.

"SHIT!" He yelled.

"I-I'm sorry! I-I didn't mean to-" Aiden cut me off when he slammed his hands on the bed. My eyes thinned in fear. Don't hit me, don't hit me. I kept thinking to myself.

"I'm not going to hit you." Aiden said.

My eyes opened slightly. "What?" I whispered. "I said, I'm not going to hit you!" Aiden yelled. I flinched a little. How did he know what I was thinking? "You talk out loud." He said. All I did was nod my head and sit there, this time I made sure not to think anything.

After a couple moments of silence, Aiden spoke up. "What about our bet?" He smirked. What bet? I pondered on it for a little bit.

"Ohhh, yeah. Right, about that-" Aiden cut me inturrupted me again, but this time instead of talking he moved closer to me. He placed both hands on the sides of my head and hopped onto the bed. He hovered over me and sat on me. He locked his legs around my waist tightly and sat up slightly.

I was trapped. Oh god, what was he going to do to me! Aiden was straddling me! I wiggled and tried to get out but when I moved he only tightened his lock on me. I used my arms and attempted to push him off but he grabed them and held them above my head. I was litterally stuck!

"WHAT ARE YOU DOING?" I yelled.

Aiden yelled back "SHUT UP! I'M NOT EVEN HURTING YOU!" I stopped yelling, I guess he was right, he wasn't hurting me but come on! When you have your worst nightmare sitting on your waist it's kind of scary.

"What do you want!" I gulped.

"I won the bet, so I'm getting what I want." Aiden sat up and let go of my hands. He placed his hands on my sides and rubbed his thumbs in small circles.

"Fine, what do you want, since you won." I said and Aiden smiled. Again, with his smiles. Why am I seeing them so frequently? Aiden leaned in towards me and got dangerously close to my face. He then turned his head and headed towards my neck. What was he doing?

I felt something warm and incredibly soft on my skin. It was almost like a kiss. A slight kiss. Another one was made but slighty different, a little more agressive. It felt really good. Aidens thumbs moved slightly faster and his breathing changed a little. I could feel something poke me a little, bit I ignored it. I placed my hands on his stomach and unconsciously tried to get him closer to me. Aiden growled. Aiden kept kissing my neck slowly and then more aggressively. Alternating between each kiss. Then he bit me. HE BIT ME!

"S-Seriously! You're giving me a h-hickey?!" I nearly said in one sentence. Aiden sucked my neck harder and bit once more. I almost let out a gasp. While he kissed my neck for the last time his thumbs came to a slow stop and his breathing slowed down slightly. He backed his hands off of my body and placed them on his thighs. All his weight was on my hips, and boy was he heavy. Aiden got off me slowly, his face was red. He fixed his shorts and straightened his shirt.

"Well, that was fun." He smirked. "Let's have another bet soon, kay?"

Chapter 3 - You @ Aiden's house

A couple days passed since Aiden did that to me and all I've done is ignore him. I've avoided him like my life depended on it. Unfortunately, he was in my gym class and math class. Aiden was also my best friends brother so there was no avoiding him all together. Today after school I was going to hang out with Louis. I loved his house because it was so spacious compared to mine.

It was after school and I getting a ride from Louis. I saw him next to his Hummer and waved at him. "Hey man!" I exlaimed.

Louis looked awkwardly. "I'm sorry about this..." He opened the door and the pointed to the back seat. I looked in the back of his car cautiously. There he was, Aiden.

I slammed the door shut and yelled at Louis. "WHAT THE HELL MAN? DON'T YOU KNOW I'M AVOIDING HIM?"

All Louis could do was shrug his shoulders and say "I'm sorry, he need a ride. I already told Aiden to be good to you and leave you alone."

I groaned out loud and slowly entered the Hummer. I got into the front seat and prayed that he wouldn't say anything to me, let alone beat me up. Even though he did what he did at the nurse's office, he's still a bully. Louis got in the drivers seat and he pulled out of the schools parking lot. I could feel his eyes on the back of my head. He would cough occasionally and the hair's on my neck would stand up. Goodness, I was scared of him.

Soon we approached Louis and Aiden's house. I quickly got out of the car and ran inside to their house. Of course, out of my luck, the door was locked. I hit the door and looked back pleading that Louis would be right next to me. Nope, It was Aiden."I'm not going to do anything to you, Louis said if I did he'd destory everything in my room." Aiden said while fumbling for the house keys. Our hands brushed against each others. I quickly backed my hand away from him and turned my body the other way so I wouldn't see him anymore. Finally, he unlocked the door. I rushed inside and ran up the stairs to Louis's room.

A couple hours later I was hungry. I decided to go down to the kitchen and find anything consumable to eat. I looked through all the cabinets and found nothing. I turned my eyes to the one cabinet that I haven't touched. It was Aidens cabinet. No one was allowed to touch that. My stomach growled. I have two options, be a ninja and steal some of Aidens food, holding on to dear life that I won't be caught or leave the room and let myself starve.

Forget option B, I'm going with being a ninja. I quickly run up to the wooden cabinet and swing the door open as fast as I could. I scanned the shelves for anything edible. Oreo's, My favorite. I grabbed the package and flung myself to the fridge to get a glass of milk. You can't have Oreo's without milk. I dunked one Oreo and started at my second.

I heard foot steps behind me and a strong grip slide through my arms inbetween my elbows and my body. I could feel a mysterious hard figure behind me, resting on my back. It leaned in. "Well, look what we have here." The mysterious voice whispered in my ear. Shivers went down my spine. I knew it was Aiden, I could tell by his voice.

I turned to face Aiden, his arm still wrapped around me. Aiden grabbed the Oreo out of my hand and took another bite of it. He licked his lips and made a moan. "That was almost as good as our bet." He mumbled. "Of course, you're better." I could feel him smirk against my neck.

I forced myself out of Aidens grip and pushed him against the counter. I placed both hands on the sides of him. "I never knew you liked it rough, but isn't this a little fast?" Aiden smirked. I mentally faced palmed myself, what was I doing. Aiden grabbed my wrists that were pinning him down. He turned us around so I was the one being captured. Of course, how couldn't I see this coming.

"What do you want?" I growled at him.

Aiden wiped away the left over cookie crumbs forming on my lip. He licked his thumb and the crumb that was on it. "I want my Oreo's back." He said sweetly.

Chapter 4 - All because of Oreo's.

"Back off of me Aiden." I glared at him. I shoved Aiden backwards till he reached the counter. Aiden was completely dumbfounded, his eyes were widened and his mouth loosened. "Where did that burst of confidence come from?" He pushed me backwards against the original counter. "Maybe, it's because you ate MY oreo's or is it because of the moment we shared together?" Aiden let his finger roam my chest, zig zagging. My body stiffened. I shifted slightly and Aiden clutched my wrists. I clenched my teeth. "Let me go." Aiden squeezed tighter. "Now." I snapped. I struggled out of his firm grasp. Aiden took a step closer, in till our bodies were touching. "No." He claimed. "I want my oreo's back and I'll make sure I get them back." I hissed at him. His eyes got darker. "I love it when you get angry." Aiden released my wrists and I attempted to punch his arm but he jumped out of the way. I made anther attempt to punch him but he avoided it again. He ran to the other side of the room. I followed him, furiously. By this time I was on a rampage to punch him. How dare he think that? How dare him! Aiden jumped up on the couch that was in the living room. I reached for a pillow and aimed at Aidens head. Instead of hitting him in the head, I hit his chest. Aiden flinched and made a grunt noise. Serves him right. I smirked. "Ethan, you are so dead." Aiden roared. Aiden grabbed the nearest pillow and smacked me right in the head. I tumbled onto the ground. As I was scrambling to get up, Aiden thew his pillow and toppled over me. We began to wrestle each other. Of course, I was loosing. I was struggling to keep him off of me but soon gave up. Aiden sat on me. "Get off of me, you fatty!" I yelped. "You're crushing me!" I wiggled my body so he would get off of me but he didn't budge. He only tightened his grip and it seemed as if he even got heavier. "Aiden!" I whined. I put my hands on his chest and pushed. Aiden flinched slightly but didn't move. When I placed my hands on his chest he changed. Aiden grabbed my hands and slowly lowered them down his body. I couldn't move. What was he doing? Aiden moved my hands down to his stomach. How far was he going to go? Suddenly, one of my hands was under his shirt. I could feel his soft skin. Aiden shifted my hands to his sides. His grip loosened when I wiggled my fingers. I could hear a faint sounds coming from him. My eyes widened. What was that sounds? Aiden continued to move my hands up and down his sides. More sounds came from him. Oh god! He's not turning into a monster, right? Aiden placed my hands on his stomach and let go of them. I couldn't help but smirk when I felt his defined abs. I traced my fingers over them. Aiden's mouth opened and he groaned. "Did you just moan?" I panicked. Aiden's face was beat red. " Are you blush-" "What in the world are you two doing?!" Louis walked towards us. Our faces turned towards Louis. "You're not beating Ethan up are you!?" Louis's face was scary. He shoved Aiden off me. "What did I tell you Aiden! No bothering Ethan!" Aiden didn't say anything. His face was still red but not as bad as before. All Aiden did was stare at me. "Leave!" Louis yelled at Aiden. Aiden ran upstairs and slammed his door. What in the world just happened?

Chapter 5 - Tension

The next morning was extremely awkward. Aiden, Louis and I all sat around the rounded table while their mother cooked a pankcake feast. There was never enough food, especially around three boys. I wasn't hungry this morning because of the events last night. This morning was overwhelming and I hated every minute of it it.

All of a sudden and out of nowhere, Louis screamed, "AIDEN! STOP STARING AT EATHEN! YOU CREEP!" The atmosphere took a toll for the worse. Aiden clenched his fork and made stabbing motions towards his brother.

"I was not staring at him, you freak!" Aiden lashed backwards. "I was simply spacing-out and his fatass happened to be in the way," He groaned slightly and forced his head down and angrly tore at his pancakes. I couldn't help but little out a snort, what a child. "What are you laughing at fatass?" He snapped.

I think my jaw just dropped a little, to be so direct, especially in the morning. "Uh, nothing." I said quietly and played with my fork. My eyes peeked out slightly and noticed Aiden gazing at me. 'I guess Louis was right, he was staring at me.' I whispered, barely audiable.

Knowing my luck, Aiden heard and fuzed up. He slammed his fork down on his plate and turned his entire body towards me. I didn't expect Aiden to give a reaction that great. "Listen nerd, I was not and never will stare at you." Aiden said half-heartedly. A slight pang hit my chest, my face hardened. Could he be serious?

Louis, witnessing all of this, nervously spoke "Are you two dating or something?" He laughed, "The tension between the two of you is incredible. I can see the bolts of lightning sparking." Louis quickly motioned his hands back and forth between us, as if there was bolts flying off of each other. "OW! YOU ZAPPED ME!" He chuckeled.

Aiden yelled "Zap off, We're not dating. We're more of enemies." But after Aiden said that his face was filled with regret.

Chapter 6 - Deep shades of red

M onday has arrived and I dreaded every minute of it, mostly because of Aidens angry clan of unintellegent and foolish minions. Instead of doing something himself, he would tell one of his stupid "friends" to do it for him, they're basically dogs. I couldn't help but smile thinking of one of his friends" barking at Aiden.

"What are you laughing at stupid?" One of Aidens minions said while slamming my head into one of the nearby lockers. I could litterally feel my head and the locker mold into one, I think my head might have left a dent. Poor kid who has to have this locker now, oh well.

"Nothing, don't worry about it." I chirped and attempted to escape. Unfortunatly, I didn't manage to flee and was thrown against the lockers roughly. Now, that's going to leave a mark. He punched my face, leaving a brused mark for later and possibly a bloody lip. He tossed me onto the ground and started to kick me against the lockers.

I supposed it was more painful than ususal especially since the recent beatings have stopped a little. The beatings didn't last long because I was interupted by the ruler himself, Aiden.

"That's enough." His face tightned when he saw me. I was probally bleeding all over and had marks all over my body. "Leave him." His minion left without another word.

Aiden stayed back for just a second, his faced changed from anger to concern. Aiden looked concerned? Maybe becuase of my appearence, he might have felt a little concerned, maybe.

Chapter 7 - The bully

One of the most dreaded part of the day arrived. Gym. I was honestly starting to dislike gym now. I mean, now that everything is happening with me and Aiden.. I just don't know what to think anymore.

I entered the locker room and headed towards my normal lonley corner. People tended to avoid this area of the room, they might get picked on. I tore off my shirt and opened my locker. Something was weird. I heard snickering in the background.

"Missing something?" One of Aidens friends says waving my gym shirt in his hands. I quickly turned around and ran after him. I chased him into the bathroom. He turned the sink on and shoved my shirt under the running water.

"NOOOO!" I shouted. The boy laughed at my reaction. I sprinted towards the sink and grabbed my shirt out as fast as humanly possible. It was soaked. I glared at him, a real death glare. All he did was smile. I didn't know what to do, I didn't have another shirt to wear.

"I guess you can go home now." He chuckled. "leave and take your pathetic shirt with you." He crossed his arms and headed towards the door. "Nobody want's you here." He left the room.

I guess that's one way to tell someone you don't like them. I leaned against the wall with my soaking wet shirt in my hand. Now what am I supposed to do?

Chapter 8 - Aidens smell

I was straining my shirt inbetween my thoughts. Should I leave? What do I do about my shirt? I don't have another.. My hand curled up into a fist. I seriously hate Aiden and his stupid jerks he bothers to call his friends. I'm so done with him right now. I can't stand him.

Only then, just my luck, Aiden walks into the room. He stands there and takes a deep breath. I wonder what happened, wait no I don't. I don't care about him. Aiden walks over to the sink and stares into the mirror, completely ignoring the fact that I'm not wearing a shirt or the fact that my gym shirt is soaked in my hands. It doesn't really matter.

After a few moments, he turns and realizes that I'm awkwarly watching him. My face turns abit red and I feel like I've been caught doing something bad. "Hi.." I mumbled, lifting my hand a little bit.

He pauses, his eyes travel up and down my body. Our eyes meet and his head makes a sharp turn to the right, "Why aren't y-you wearing a shirt?" He studders. I can see his slightly red face. Was he "checking me out?" Not possible. "Wait here." He said while leaving the room. Psh- Like I was going to leave. Not like this.

In a minute or two, Aiden comes back with something in his hands. A lump of clothing. He stands in front of me and holds out his hands. "Here- you can use my shirt." He mumbles. "I've only worn it once, It's actually an extra." He grabs my hand and forces me told hold his shirt. "Put it on."

I awkwardly stood there, holding his shirt. Aiden urged me to put on his shirt. I slipped his extra gym shirt over my head. It was a size bigger than me. His shirt was almost drownding me. I brought it up to my nose, boy did it smell like sweat. "It smells terrible." I groaned.

Aiden's face brightened. "Sorry.." He scratched his neck. "It's better than that, right?" He points to the wet shirt.

"I suppose so." I didn't want to admit it but I really like his shirt. It smelled like Aiden.

Chapter 9 - Goose Bumps

I walked in to the gym with Aidens large shirt on and boy did I ever get stares. All the girls gave me glares. The boys gave me looks of envy, only because I got the girls attention.

Aiden was playing around with his group of friends but when I walked in the room they all stopped. Their mouths dropped, eyes widened. "Isn't that your shirt?" One of the boys said.

I've never felt so embarrassed, just to be wearing a shirt. I clung to the edge of the shirt, kept my head down to avoid any eye contact and quietly walked over to Louis.

Louis looked extremely shocked, almost terrified. "Is that my brothers shirt your wearing?" I could only nod my head slightly. A group of girls and a couple guys came over to us. "Why are you wearing that shirt?!" Someone chirped. "Isn't that Aidens shirt?" A boy whispered.

I had no words. I was in panic mode with all the unwanted attention I was getting. "I- uh..." I lifted my head. "Um.. My.." I almost started choking. I couldn't breathe.

"He needed a shirt to borrow and I let him use mine." Aiden stepped in behind me and wrapped his arm around my shoulders. "Now everyone go back to doing whatever you were doing and leave him alone." I could feel Aidens warmth radiating onto me. His torso was pressed against my back and chills came over me. We're so close I got goosebumps. I know we've been closer than this, so why is it affecting me this much?

Chapter 10 - Because of Aidens shirt

I can feel Aidens breath on my neck. It was warm and ragged. Aidens hand dropped from my shoulder and slightly touched my hip. "It's okay now, they'll leave you alone." He whispered in my ear and the warmth made me shiver. His hand traveled loosely and settled on my butt. He firmly grasped it. I accidentally let out a small gasp, I don't know where that came from but I know that wasn't supposed to happen.

"Aiden stop.." I tried to regain my composure but failed miserably. His hand continued towards my waistband of my pants. We are in the middle of gym class and he's doing this to me! "Aiden stop." I attempted with a little more force. "But you're so cute." Aiden whispered under his breath just barely audible. Aiden hand backed off very reluctantly. "Fine" he pouted while sticking his lower lip out.

During the rest of the class I could feel everyone's eyes stare at me. Class was only half over but I couldn't help but feel awkward. I tried to stay behind everyone and hide myself away in a corner but it didn't work very well. Aidens constant staring wasn't helping either. I couldn't stand it anymore! I asked the teacher to use the bathroom but really I was going to ditch.

I quickly exited the gym and almost tripped on a tile. I was so flustered. I needed to clear my head from all these weird thoughts. I stomped over to my corner and stripped off Aidens shirt as fast as possible. I crumpled it up and threw it on the bench in front of me. "Stupid Aiden and his stupid shirt!" I cursed at the crumpled pile. I crossed my arms and kicked the bench.

"Well, isn't this a site to see." A voice from behind me chuckled. "A pouting, half-naked Ethan."

Chapter 11 - Sorta kiss (Aidens POV)

✱ ***AIDENS POV****

God, I wanted to touch him.

His beautiful body.

I couldn't stand not being able to touch him. Ethan looked especially hot today because he was wearing my shirt. MY shirt. He would look even better not wearing a shirt. I couldn't help but smile at the thought.

I walked in the locker room and I see Ethan pouting in his corner. Thank goodness I skipped class. I get to spend it with Ethan now. I smile as I noticed that he kicked the bench.

Oh lord, was that adorable. I wish I could do things to that boy! I chuckle. "Well, isn't this a site to see." I take in Ethan's broad shoulders as they stiffen from my voice. "A pouting, half-naked Ethan." I say sexually.

I step closer to Ethan and his breath sharpens. "Don't move." Our backs are touching. I can feel his rough skin against my shirt. Just knowing that our skin is almost touching makes me excited.

I place my palm on his shoulder and trace over one of his scars. "I'm so sorry." I say quietly.

"Why are you sorry?" Ethan says back. His head turns slightly and our eyes make contact.

"For everything... and for this." I leaned over and place a gentle kiss on the mark.

I looked up and see Ethan's eyes. There filled with terror, confusion, and a little something else.

I looked at Ethan's lips. I want to kiss him. He subconsciously licks them. I look into Ethan's eyes, then back at his lips. I really wanted to kiss him. I leaned in closer and Ethan's breathing became ragged.

God, I wanted to kiss him.

Chapter 12 - Kiss me

Aiden wrapped one of his arms around my waist. His arm touching my bare body. His other hand rested against my stomach; caressing it. I can feel his hot breath on the back of my neck and I'm getting goose bumps and I involuntarily gasp.

"Ethan." Aiden pauses. "I want you." He softly bites my ear. "I want to kiss you more than will ever know."

I froze. My breath got shorter and shorter and I felt like I was going to faint. What is happening to me? All he was doing was touching me... That's what was happening to me; he was touching me! His hand gradually lowered, brushing against the hem of my shorts. "You're so sexy. I can't stand it."

Aidens breath was on fire. I could feel his desire. His chest pressed against me, leaving no space for anything. I could clearly feel what was happening to him.

I reached for Aidens hands trying to lift them off me but he latched on tighter. "I'll only let you go under one condition."

I tried clawing at his arms. He wouldn't let go. I groaned loudly in annoyance, not afraid for him to hear. "What?"

"Kiss me."

Chapter 13 - Kissing Aiden Pt. 1

"**K**iss me and I'll let you go." Aiden demanded as he squeezed tighter.

"Fine!" I yelled. Our body heat was making me dizzy.

Aiden let go of me, and I whipped around. Our faces were inches away. Aidens face was bright red with blush. Trapping me in; he extended his arms, so they touched the lockers. My face flushed. "There's no escaping this." He smirked.

I groaned and inwardly cried. I took a deep breath to prepare myself. I leaned in closer and ever so slightly, I pecked his lips. "There! There's you go! Thats your kiss! Now let me go!" I grabbed his arms but he didn't move.

Aiden sighed. "That's not a kiss, that's a bump on the mouth." He took a deep breath and exhaled. "Let me show you how it's done."

Aiden lets go of that wall and grabs my waist hard. He pushed us against the wall. Our body's touching each other. I could feel everything and I'm sure he could too.

Aidens head tilted and his eyes pierced into mine. His gaze was so strong. I looked at his bright red lips. They were gradually getting lower and closer to mine when they finally crashed into mine. It was rough and hard, filled with all of his emotions. I could hear his muffled moans. His hands went to my head to lock me in place. So I wouldn't move. He tugged on my hair.

"Kiss me back." He said breathlessly. He kissed and sucked my neck. "I want you to kiss me back."

Chapter 14 - Kissing Aiden Pt. 2

My body was on fire. I couldn't deny the sensation I was getting down below. Aiden just looked really hot with a flushed face and bruised lips. I couldn't help it but admire how strong he was and how good he was at kissing.

"Kiss me back." He said breathlessly. He kissed and sucked my neck. "I want you to kiss me back."

Oh goodness, now he was kissing and sucking my neck. I unintentionally let out muffled noises letting Aiden know how amazing him kissing me felt.

Aiden sucked and licked right below my ear. I moaned even louder. DANG IT. He found my weak spot! I could feel Aiden smile against my skin when he bit down. My head jolted back giving him even more access. Every kiss was making me melt inside and out.

"Aiden." I choked out. Aiden stopped kissing and looked at me. Flushed and bruised with a dazed look. This was not helping the problem below. Aidens eyes, they gave off.. Desire. Lust. Passion. Need.

Aiden placed his lips back onto mine. His kiss was delicate and softer than last. "Kiss.." He lifted his lips and placed them back. "Me." Lifting them again. "Back." He waited.

I did the impossible. I raised my head slightly and kissed him back.

---HELLO EVERYONE. DID YOU ENJOY? Please leave a comment and vote for my story!!

Q; What's your favorite weather?

A; RAIN!! A light storm, not a deathly one.

Chapter 15 - What now?

I looked Aiden in the eyes, leaned up and kissed him. It was beautiful and slightly awkward at the same time. Who would have thought that kissing Aiden would be almost the scariest thing I've ever experienced. I was used to the surprise beatings but this was something even God didn't plan.

We stood there for a moment, not moving. Aiden didn't move. His lips were rough but they were everything that I expected and more. My hands started to shake and I slowly backed away but Aiden didn't allow me to. Instead, he got closer. He reached for my hands and carefully intertwined them together.

He whispered, "thank you" and gave a little smile. "I've been waiting for that for way to long."

All I could do was smile back.

"Now what?" I asked awkwardly. Our hands intertwined and our bodies mangled together.

Aiden let out a chuckle. He took a step back. The air between us gave me goosebumps. It was cold now that he wasn't on me.

"Ethan." He paused, contemplating what he was going to say. My face was pure red, I could just feel my body heating up. "Will you go-"

The doors slammed open and kids flooded in. I didn't know what to do. I panicked and threw his hands and shoved him away. I slid my shirt on and ran.

I didn't know where I'm running. I just knew that I had to. I really wish I didn't but I did.

I was too caught up in the moment. I was all hot and bothered and I'm sure he was too. We were being irrational, that's all it was.

I slow down and scratch my head. Yeah, irrational. I'm sure he didn't really feel anything. How could he? I feel my face harden. It's me we're talking about. Ethan, the kid he picks on. --HELLO EVERYONE. DID YOU ENJOY? Please leave a comment and vote for my story!!

Q; who's your favorite actor/actress?

A; Keria Kneightly

Chapter 16 - I need him. (Aidens POV)

✱ *****AIDENS POV*******

Ethan smiled at me. He was so amazing, words couldn't describe how I feel right now. Finally, after months of secretly loving him I finally have the courage to ask him out.

I chuckled and took a step back. "Ethan." His face blushed red. I almost died of how cute that was. I could eat him up this second. I opened my mouth. "Will you go-"

I stopped. Doors slammed open. Kids piled in the room. Class wasn't supposed to end yet, what happened?!

Ethan let go of my hands and pushed me back. WAIT! I panicked. My legs wouldn't move. "Etha-" I tried to mouth out. I stood frozen.

One of my friends slapped my back. "Whatcha doing" He paused and turned "why's your face bright red?" He asked mockingly. He looks around to see Ethan running out the door. "Hanging with lover boy?" He laughed. "I always knew you had a thing for him."

What. "You knew..?" I questioned. He laughs harder.

"Of course I knew. You stare at him everyday." He picks at his finger. "Every. Single. Day."

I blush. I must have really liked Ethan. No, I really do like Ethan. I think about Ethan almost every day. His soft kissable lips. His perfect ass that I just want to squeeze. I need to stop before I get to excited.

"Get that stupid smile off your face. It's grossing me out." My friend shivers. "Where is he?" He looks around.

SHIT. Sudden realization sets in and I panic. CRAP. Ethan! Where did he go?! I run out of the room and frantically look around.

I run to Ethans next classroom and look through the window. He's not there. It's almost lunch time, I run to the cafeteria. He's not there either! I'm getting very nervous. I pulled on my hair. Why can't I find him! I'll give it one more shot. His locker.

I need to find him.

I need him!---HELLO EVERYONE. DID YOU ENJOY? Please leave a comment and vote for my story!!

Q; Fruits or Vegetables

A: Fruits all the way!!!!

Chapter 17 - I'm secretly a model.

✱ ** ETHANS POV****

I honestly don't know why I ran away. My body was reacting so strongly towards him.

I looked around. Where am I? "GOSH DANGIT. WHY AM I SO DUMB?!" I yelled in frustration.

I kicked the wall. "SHIT!" Pain was rushing through my foot into my leg. I give up and leaned against the wall. Eventually sliding on to the floor. Sitting down, I heavily sighed.

"Ethan?" The hairs on the back of my neck stood up as I instantly recognized the voice.

Scrambling to get up, I panicked. Moving my injured foot, I screamed. Quickly, I slammed my hand over my mouth, silently begging that he didn't hear me.

I tried crawling on the ground. Slowly but surely; I was going to make an exit. Secretly praying over and over that I could make it to a classroom or bathroom and just hide.

"Ethan?" The voice paused. "What in the world are you doing?"

I turned, shocked like a deer in headlights. I should have seen this coming.

Aiden had reached the hall and saw me awkwardly half-crawling on the ground mumbling gibberish.

Flipping over to my back, I put my hand behind my head and crossed my good leg over my bad. "Being a model, why?" I said awkwardly. Smooth.

Aiden just stared with a puzzled look. He leaned against the wall, crossing his arms and raising an eyebrow. "Oh really? Could you show me more?"

That backfired terribly.

Aiden looked at me with devil eyes. I knew he was up to something. "Uh. Business hours aren't open."

What type of comeback was that?!

He smiled at my response and even laughed a little. Aiden leaned off the wall and walked towards me.

I guess it was an amazing comeback. No!! Curse myself! I frowned.

I attempted to turn myself on my stomach and run-crawl away but I was stopped. Aiden stepped in front of me. Surprised, I fell on my back.

With extreme presence, Aiden stood there towering over me. I was scared. No- deep inside I was excited to see what he would do.

Staring up at Aiden was actually really thrilling but, remembering everything he's done to me.. Honestly, he can't do much worse.

Aiden bent over and sat down next to me, leaning next to me. His face was gradually getting closer and closer to mine. Without notice, his entire face was in front of mine. His eyes were staring into mine so intensely. I could feel the electricity between us. I gulped. Unknowingly, my eyes closed.

I could feel his breath on my lips. Inches away. I licked my lips. I was ready to accept my fate but when I opened my eyes slightly.

"Expecting something?" He chuckled smiling.

---HELLO EVERYONE. DID YOU ENJOY? Please leave a comment and vote for my story!!

Q: Would you rather live in a warm or cold place?

A: I would live somewhere cold cause I hate the heat!!

Chapter 18 - How much I xxxx you

✱ *** ETHANS POV ****

Was I expecting something? I opened my eyes slightly. Aidens face In front of mine. His eyes were entrancing. Why is he so hot?!

"No." I pouted, crossing my arms.

"You sure?" Aiden turned and pushed me down. I gulped, now laying on the floor. Aiden climbing on top of me so that his legs were straddling my hips. His weight was pinning me down and I couldn't move an inch.

"Get off me." I hissed, barely able to breath from the monster sitting on my stomach. I wiggled and attempted to push him, little by little. I used my right hand and placed it on his chest. I summoned my inner strength but no luck found. Aiden took this opportunity to capture my hand. His grip around my hand tightened and he pulled me forward. Closer to him.

"You silly boy." Aiden shakes his head and laughs. "You never learn do you?"

Growing afraid of what he might say next, I squirmed and tried to get away but he grips my wrists harder. It was starting to hurt. He captured both of my hands and forced them above my head.

"Learn what?" I choked out, my body stiffing. The air between us is growing more and more intense and I'm slowly getting more hot and bothered but still slightly afraid. Is this normal? I think to myself.

Half a second later, just enough to knock me out of my trance. Aiden lowers his entire body onto me so that it's barely hovering over me. I can feel him but I don't feel how much he weighs. I can feel his heart beat and it's super fast. His face is level with my neck and I can feel Aidens breath tickling the hairs. He blows out a tiny puff of air and my entire body shivers with delight. If my body wasn't happy then, it's happy now.

Aiden whispered breathlessly "I want you to learn..." He paused, adding a more dramatic effect to the situation. His hands released mine and wondered down my sides. I can feel my pants getting tighter and tighter. He's barely touching me yet I'm this excited. He reached my waist band and tugged slightly.

I completely froze, paralyzed. My senses were at its peak. I was feeling every touch he made, every breath he breathed. I reacted to his touch without evening knowing it. He kissed the side of my neck. I can't control what I'm feeling anymore. I moaned. Loudly. Aiden continued to shower my neck with kisses. Long ones, short ones. I felt every one of them.

Aidens hands were crawling all over my torso. Feeling every nook and cranny. Memorizing what it feels like as if it's never going to happen again.

He muffles in between kissing. "I want... Youu... To learnn" His kisses slow down to a stop. My neck beginning to feel bare. He lifts his head and shifts his body. His face was bright red and has shallow breathing. He looks me in the eye. Deeply. In one swift moment he says the one thing I wanted to hear.

"How much I want you." "How much I need you." "How much I lo..."

---HELLO EVERYONE!! MERRY CHRISTMAS! Did you enjoy this little special?

Q; what's one of your favorite holiday memories?

A; every year my family comes over and we all spend time together.

Chapter 19 - Because I like you.

This was it. The moment I've been waiting for. The moment of truth. The words I've been unconsciously been demanding for.

Ethan slowly kisses in between each saying. "How much I want you. How much I need you. How much I lo..." Aiden stops- mid sentence.

I panic. Why did he stop? In mid-sentence too! I frantically look around and see if something was there that made him stop. Nothing, just an empty hallway. I turned back to him, with a frightened face.

Aidens face was crimson red. I've never seen a face as red as his. His eyes were sparkling and his breathing was rapid. He was just staring at me. Intensely.

"why did you stop..?" I asked dazed and confused. Aiden backed off of me, simultaneously letting my hands free. As if it was possible, I could feel a breeze between us.

I reached out and found his arms, guiding them back down to my waist. Realizing what I had done, I let go, flustered. My body was acting on its own. It was as if Aiden was in control of me, my body and mind was completely his.

Aiden smirked and laughed. Blatantly. I was hurt. He knew that he was in control of me. He knew that I wanted him to finish his sentence. He knew that I would try to close the space between us. He knew how I felt.

"You never learn, do you?" Aiden mutters under his breath.

"What do I never learn?!" I shouted.

Aiden leaned down and kissed me on the lips.

"Did you just kiss me?" I asked dumbfounded and shocked.

Aiden bit his lip and nodded his head a little. "Of course I did!" He said proudly.

"Why..?" I couldn't accept the reality.

Aiden kissed me again and smiled sweetly. "Because I like you!"

Aiden kissed the tip of my nose.

My face was in major derp mode. My body couldn't move, not because of his body weight sitting on top of me, but because I was shocked.

Aiden just smiled. He shifted around and went to sit next to me but I stopped him.

"Where are you going?!" Clutching his shirt so he wouldn't move.

Aiden laughed. "Does my wittle Ethan not want me to leave?" He says in a baby voice.

My jaw dropped and shoved him off me. "You can leave."

"Fine." Aiden pouted. Aiden straightened up and brushed his clothes off. He stomped his foot, like a child and started to walk away.

"Wait!" I pleaded. "Can you help me?" I whispered pathetically.

Aiden stopped and turned around. "What's the magic word?" He stuck his tongue out.

I let out a deep breath. I began to batt my eyes and pout my lips. "Pweeesssseeee?" All cutesy.

Aiden let out a heavy breath. "I can never win with you, can I?"

He walked back over to me and bent over. "Get on." He pointed to his back.

"You want me to get on your back?" I asked curiously.

"No, I want to play leapfrog. Yes, I want you to get on my back." He says sarcastically.

Embarrassed, I touch his shoulders. I shift all my weight onto his back. Aiden grabs my thighs and holds me tight. I wrap my arms around his neck and pray that he won't drop me.

----------------------HELLO EVERYONE. DID YOU ENJOY THIS CHAPTER!?

Q; What is your favorite month and why? A; December because I love snow!

Chapter 20 - You're a wizard, grant me a wish

I am now being carried by Aiden. Not princess style but on his back. Holy crap. What just happened, no, what is happening?

Being carried wasn't a terrible thing but it wasn't a great thing either. I'm so embarrassed. I indirectly but directly admitted that I had feelings for him. Just perfect. This was so confusing. I went to sigh but I accidentally snorted out loud.

Sometimes life has a way of working out a way to screw you over. I think that was happening to me. Why did I get on his back. I groaned and hit my head against his shoulder. Gosh, I'm so full of noises.

Aiden reacted to my head hitting his shoulders and he yelped in pain. "What? Was that because we didn't play leap frog?!"

I hit my head on his shoulder again. Smartass.

"Alright, alright! Next time you decide to play model, we'll play leap frog too!" Aiden chuckled and re-positioned himself so he could carry me better.

----------Once we reached the nurses office, Aiden set me down on one of the chairs. He reached for my foot and examined it.

"I'm no doctor but you should probably Ice that." Aiden picks my foot up again. "Maybe?" He says in a questionable tone and shrugs his shoulders.

I dramatically gasp in disbelief and threw my hands up in the air. "Really? I would have never guessed!"

Aiden rummages through cabinets and drawers; looking for something.

"Catch!" Aiden threw something at my face. Ah, an ice pack.

"Just what I needed. Thanks for the heads up." I spat sarcastically.

"Your welcome." He said cheekily.

I grumbled some noises and put the ice pack on my leg. Hopefully, my leg will be magically healed with the power of ice. I hovered my hands over my wound and moved them around. I whispered "abracadabra".

Aiden on the other side of the room just watches me with a puzzled face. "Did you seriously just do that?"

Shoot, he saw that. I'm guilty as charged but I wont let him know that! What should I do? Run..? No.. I can't do that my leg hurts... I looked around the room and didn't find anything to help my situation.

"What are you, Harry Potter?" He laughs. "Have you been practicing spells in your free time?"

"Maybe..." I grumbled under my breath. He didn't have to know about that.

Aiden slowly walked towards me and puts his hands on my knees. "Since your a wizard, harry, how about you grant me a wish." He demands.

I turn my head slightly, not understanding the question. "What do you want?"

"You." Aiden softly kissed my lips.

I pushed Aiden back. I wasn't ready for that. Aiden frowned with the lack of contact.

"Your wish is my command. " I smiled and kissed him back.

Only once though, I can't spoil him. Not yet.

HEY EVERYONE. WHAT DID YOU GUYS THINK? MAKE SURE TO VOTE AND COMMENT!

TO MAKE THINGS MORE INTERESTING: I WANT YOUR HELP! I WANT YOU TO TELL ME WHAT YOU THINK SHOULD HAPPEN NEXT!

Guys. I don't really like calling you fans so someone please come up with a name to call us!!

Q: Do you know any foreign languages?

A: I'm fluent in english! :P I'm also learning Korean (2 years), Japanese and french.(I took French for 4 years)

Side note/

I'm sorry that I haven't made longer chapters, I'm working on that (really I am) but I don't know what to write about. I make sure I at least have more than 500 words!

(Plus, I kinda like you guys constantly commenting that you want to update. ;) Makes me feel wanted :P)

Chapter 21 - Devilish Smile

"Your wish is my command." Ethan smiles at me and kisses me.

I was so overjoyed that I couldn't contain my happiness. I squealed. I don't think I've ever made that sound in my life. Oh my gosh.

We kissed for a moment, then he pulled away. I frowned at the lack of contact. "Come back.." I whispered, my eyes peeking open.

Instead of kissing, Ethan was staring at me. Devilishly. That's weird, usually I'm the one who makes that face. Right? I had to think about that for a second but gave him a confused look instead. I tried to match his devilish look but miserably failed.

Ethans devilish smile deepened as he got closer to me. He gently touched my leg. I was getting nervous. He's never taken the initiative. It was always me who took the first step.

Ethan kept getting closer. His hand went up my shirt, gently touching my sides and landed on my shoulder.

He was tracing my shoulder up and down with his finger. Humming "Should I..?" He titled his head. "Should I not..?" He was using his finger instead of a flower.

I was so badly confused and slightly turned on that I didn't know how to act or feel.

So I just sat there and let Ethan take me.

**************** ETHANS POV *************

I was gently stroking his arm up and down with just my finger. I was internally and externally debating whether to do anything.

I pressed down harder and widened the area I was stroking. I continued. Rubbing his shoulder, his upper arm, his elbow, his lower arm and I finally stopped at his wrist.

The tension was growing. I grabbed his wrist forcefully and pulled him onto my lap. Aiden made a noise I never heard of, almost like the sound before, like a squeal.

"Woah!" Aiden gasped as he situated himself onto me.

Aiden was definitely comfortable on my lap. I could feel everything especially what was going on in his pants.

I made eye contact and he shivered with what seemed to be excitement. I daringly moved my head closer and blew on his neck.

I smirked and went down to kiss his neck. I used my tongue to lick and bit down slightly. I was doing something dangerous.

I was giving Aiden a hickey. I was giving Aiden a mark, letting everyone know that he was taken. I was letting everyone know he was mine.

I continued to kiss his neck, gradually moving upwards to his jawline. In between kisses, I bit a couple more times, each getting harder and harder. I knew Aiden was feeling it and enjoying it because I could hear that he was moaning like no other.

Aiden started to sway on my lap, bucking his hips, trying to get as close as possible.

"Ethan.." He moaned loudly. "I need you... So badly..." He rocked faster.

I was completely out of my mind. The guy I liked confessed to me and now we're humping each other. I was so turned on, it hurt.

I kissed the corner of his lips but Aiden wasn't having it anymore. He grabbed my head and titled it, shoving his tongue down my throat. We both were moaning.

Aidens hand slid down from my head to my shoulders and finally to my hips. He slipped his fingers under my shirt and caressed the skin, feeling everything and anything he could.

--YAY THANK YOU FOR READING! WHAT DID YOU GUYS THINK? MAKE SURE TO VOTE AND COMMENT!!

Q; How tall are you? :D?A; I'm 5"6' woo!!

Side note/ I used to be 5"4' and hate it but I grew 1.5 inches over the years and grew .5 inch last month! Im late bloomer but I'm so happy!

Chapter 22 - Just Happened

 ******** ETHANS POV ************

Aiden was taking his time; taking my shirt off and feeling the skin underneath. His hands glided upwards, caressing each section until he finally got to a part he desired. He touched the area around my neck and drawing out more desire from me. I was dying to be touched.

My shirt was off already off and now it felt like it was his turn. My demanding streak was starting to ware off but I had one last demand. "Take it off." All Aiden could do was smile and obediently obey me. I bit my lip, shyly checking him out.

Aiden touched my shoulder with his hands, all the way down to my hips, caressing everything on the way. "You're so beautiful." he whispers between his heavy breathing.

I shyly looked away, suddenly all embarrassed, letting it all soak in. In that moment, when it all sunk in, I realized what's been happening for the last couple minutes. I can't believe what I did. What I've done. I took the lead! I never take the lead! I choked in my own disbelief.

Aiden kissed my cheek. "What's wrong?" He asks concerned. I feel like a baby. Like I'm backing down from being the leader, but I couldn't help it. I was so embarrassed. Aiden kissed my other cheek, trying to get an answer out of me, constantly asking what was wrong with me.

Something snapped. Honestly, I don't know what was wrong. Why was I so embarrassed? What's wrong with taking the lead? Everything was going great and I was enjoying it. Maybe a little too much? Maybe the spur of the moment passed by? Aiden was kissing my cheeks, gradually getting closer to my lips. "Wait.." I choke out. Aiden continues to get closer and closer. He never stops.

"Stop.." I try to say louder. A wild kissing Aiden was very hard to stop. I tried to move my arms to get him to stop but he didn't. "Stop!" I cried out. I used everything I had to push him away from me. A bit of distance was between us now.

Instead of relief, Aiden looked hurt. Really hurt. "What...happened?" He asked anxiously, his thumbs fiddling with each other. He looked shocked. He was so surprised that he backed off me and went to stand across the room. "Do you.." He paused, taking a deep breath, almost choking up. "Hate me now?" Aiden looked like he was about to cry. I didn't know what to do to make everything right.

"What..?" I cautiously asked. "No... I" I stood up and slowly limp-walked over to him. I stopped directly in front of him and reached for his hands. "Don't hate you." I tried to give a reassuring smile.

"Then why did you stop..?" Aiden whimpered, feeling abandoned. He turned his head to the side so I couldn't see him pout. He looked kinda cute, but in a sad way.

"I didn't mean to.. " I tried to move his head to face mine. "It just happened." Our eyes locked in together, his more hurt than mine.

"What do you mean... you didn't mean to?" He asked confused. "It just happened." Aiden asked more demanding than usual. "It doesn't just happen." His body moving closer and his voice sounding angrier. Aiden grabbed my wrists forcefully, his gaze getting darker and not the good type of dark.

His grasp around my wrists were getting tighter and tighter by the second, but I didn't dare say anything, intill Aiden started to scare me. "It hurts." I muttered under my breath, trying not to upset him more.

Realizing what he did, he dropped my wrists instantly. Aidens eyes cleared up and appeared sadder. "I'm so sorry." He pleaded. "I didn't realize what I was doing." He was apologizing profusely.

"It's fine, now you understand." I rubbed my wrists. "It just happened."

HEY EVERYBODY! WHAT DID YOU THINK? Yes, I know it wasn't exactly what you thought it would be but I think it turned out alright. I wanted more 'drama'.... I guess? What did you guys think? Did you like it? Hate it? Please let me know! Feedback! :D Actually, wait don't. I'm scared to know.

Please remember to vote and comment! <3

Q: Who is your favorite person and why?

A: My moms my favorite because she's so supportive and is willing to put up with me.

What are your plans for mothers day? Anything special?

Side note/ please don't be mad at me cause I made them do that. It just happened.

Chapter 23 - YES!

"I'm sorry, it's just happening to fast." I awkwardly said. I was worried that Aiden would hate me. "Can we take it slow?" I looked up at him, just barely enough to see his nose. I couldn't look him in the eyes.

Aiden sighed, "Yes, we can take it slow." He reached out to hug me. "It's just.. I want you so badly." He whispered. "I can't imagine a second without you."

I squeezed him tightly, "I want you too but..." My voice trailed off when my head collided into his chest. Aiden looked emotionally hurt.

Aiden hugged me tighter, rubbing my back. "Don't say anything else... I understand." He let me go and but our hands wouldn't leave each others. "How about we go on a date?" He smiled, our hands lightly swaying. "Start off slow and work our way up?"

I couldn't contain my smile. I nodded my head up and down, vigorously. "YES!" I yelped. I lightly pecked him on his cheek. Starting off slow, I reminded myself. "How about we go to a roller skating rink?" I asked exited.

Aiden looked worried but I guess Aiden couldn't let me down so he agreed. "It's a date." He grins.

It's been couple days and the day was finally here. It was date night. I was so exited, I couldn't contain my happiness. I jumped up and down in my bedroom. I was supposed to go over to Aidens house and then we're supposed to go to a roller skating.

I picked out my nicest but most mobile clothing I had. I mean, we were going roller skating. I styled my hair nicely and then messed it up. I can't look to nice on the first date, can I? Wouldn't that ruin everything? Oh my gosh, was I nervous? I thought I was just excited... I took a deep breath and smiled. "It's going to be okay."

When I arrived at Aidens house, Louis opened the door. We both looked at each other for a second, blankly. "What are you doing here?" Louis asked.

"What, a friend can't come over?" I replied while slapping his arm. I entered the house like it was mine. I've known Louis basically my whole life, so it was natural to come over.

I went into his living room and sat on one of his couches. Louis looked over at me cautiously. "Why are you dressed up?" He started scanning my body for clues.

"What is this, Sherlock Holmes?" I laughed. "Can't a guy dress up?" Louis looked at me suspiciously.

Just a second later, Aiden came down the stairs. We our eyes locked and we just stared at each other for what seemed like eternity.

"Oh I see what this is.." Louis spat, pointing at us.

"Thanks for the input, Captain Obvious." Aiden barks back at his brother. "He's mine." Aiden commands.

I couldn't help but blush.

"When did this happen?" Louis grumpily asks. "He's actually mine." He mumbles, barely audible under his breath.

Aiden punched Louis shoulder, aggressively. "Shall we go?" Aiden curiously asks me.

"Yeah." I say awkwardly, not sure of what to do. Is Louis mad at something?

WOO! HEY EVERYBODY! HOW'S IT GOING? WHAT DID YOU THINK? Got that typical love triangle going on. Hope you don't mind. :3

Q; What's your favorite animal? A: Llamas!! Sheep's!

Chapter 24 - Roller Skate Date

We arrived at the roller skating rink and I was trembling. I know that I suggested this but I never actually thought it through. I don't even know if Aiden could use roller skates! I'm so inconsiderate! I attempted to groan in my head but I guess I groaned out loud.

"What's wrong?" Aiden asks as we're walking into the entrance. I shook my head like nothing was wrong as he held open the door for me. He waits for me to pass him and I smiled greatly. What a gentleman!

We walked up to the counter. "I never asked you... but do you know how to skate?" I asked nervously, worried about the answer. The lady behind the window took our money and our shoes and replaced them with roller skates.

"There's only one way to find out." He smirks and happily runs over to one of the benches. How cute! I shuffled right next to him.

We put our skates on, making sure that they fit. Aiden struggled more than I did. Once I tied my skates, I stood up and skated around for a minute, getting a feel from the blades. This is all second nature since I've skated a couple times.

I'm doing great but Aiden on the other hand is doing terribly. Aiden was still tying his skates. I glided over to him and bent down on my knees. I reached over and grabbed his laces. "Didn't anyone ever teach you how to tie your shoes?" I laughed.

Once I finished, Aiden stood up for a good three seconds and fell over, lading on his butt. "Aiden, what in the world are you doing down there?" I asked laughing.

Aiden quickly stood up but fell over again. "I'm just testing gravity." He awkwardly spouts. He gets up, covering his face, trying to hide the blush on his face. "And the conclusion?" I questioned him, trying not to laugh.

"Works pretty darn well." He coughs and tries to maintain his balance.

"Maybe, I can help you?" I reach to hold his hand. "You know, not that there's anything wrong with gravity...." We both smiled and laughed. Aiden nods his head and grabs my hand.

We slowly skate-walked towards the roller skating rink wall. Aiden was going so slow, it was killing me. I mean, It was amazingly cute to watch him but seriously? Boy, needs to learn! And fast!

Aiden wobbled over to the wall and latched on for his life. He looked embarrassed. "I'm sorry that I suck so much."

"I'm sorry that I didn't ask if you knew how to skate.." I told him apolog etically."I should have known better."

I reached for Aidens hand and tugged him to get off the wall. "Let's try to make you better." I smiled softly. All Aiden did was comply with me.

We skated for a little bit. After a while, Aiden started getting better and gained some confidence for skating and didn't suck as much. "LOOK! I'm good at this now!" He smiled more often and even laughed. In a matter of a second, Aiden lost his balance and feel backwards onto his butt. He pouted and patted his butt.

"You got to cocky." I smirked. "At least I'm better than you at something!" I laughed.

Aiden scrambled to the wall and tried to get up. Multiple times. "That's not all your good at." Aiden smirked.

We skated for a little longer and decided it was time to get some food. We returned our skates at the counter and headed out to a pizza shack. It was really hard walking on the ground without wheels under me. I got so used to it, it just feels wrong now.

We followed a server to a booth in the back corner of the restaurant. We were put in a secluded area and there was music playing in the background so no one could hear us. Perfect for a first date. I giggled.

We ordered a couple slices of pizza and some drinks. At first we talked about what we were going to order but now, it's awkward. Aiden was blushing and I didn't know why. "It's our first date.." Aiden giggled.

I gave a strange face to him that he immediately stopped smiling. His normal stone face took over. That's the Aiden everyone else knows. "I like the nice Aiden better." I said informatively. "He's cuter." I said without thinking. Aiden turned his head sharply to look at me and I shoved a slice of pizza in my mouth.

"OH really..?" He said seductively. He placed his hand on my thigh. "Are you sure, I'm not more than that?" His hand started getting higher. My breathing fastened. Aiden leaned in and whispered in my ear. "Aren't I ..." He blew hot air slowly. "Hot?" His lips touched my ear, just barely enough to feel his teeth grazing against my ear. His hand continued to get higher and higher until he stopped. Right below of where I needed it to be.

I placed my hand on Aidens. "Not today, you're aren't." I smiled and removed his hand.

Aiden sighed. "When will I?"

I smiled. "Some day." I picked up a slice of pizza and shoved it in Aidens face. "Just not today." Aiden chewed reluctantly.

After we ate for a while, it was time to go home. Aiden stopped in front of my house and got out of the car to open the door for me. "Thanks." I say.

Aiden waves his hand in the air sadly. "I'll miss you."

---Hey guys! I just wanted to thank each and every one of you for reading my book, It really means a lot. I think it's been an amazing trip seeing how each chapter progresses into the next. I'm writing this because I hit my first milestone, 1K followers. It might not be a lot for others, but It means a lot to me, because without you guys, this book wouldn't have progressed this much. I just wanted to let you know that I have other books that need some love too. They are both Boy x Boy so It's in the same genera. I would love If you guys could read that one too! :) I'd really appreciate it! :D

I also made this chapter twice as longer than my normal chapters to thank you for being here and supporting me. I want to test out something, if you read any of my other books, I want you to leave a comment that say something weird like "The Bully sent me here!" or "I read or "I read Bully & His Crush!" I'd love to see if you actually read this and read my other books! <3

And as always, the question of the chapter! Q; Do you have any pet peeves? A; I HATE it when people waste plastic bags, like jeesh. Pack it in one bag not three! I don't need a separate bag for chips!

Chapter 25 - I warned you.

A couple days passed by and I really haven't seen Aiden around. I've talked with Louis a bit but that's about it. What's this feeling? I pouted as I walked to gym class.

I walked over to my locker and began to change my outfit. I looked around to see if Aiden was around. No luck. I mumbled to myself "What is going on..." Where is he? Did I do something wrong on our date?

I passed through the gym doors and began to stretch in my normal spot. Louis walked over and began stretching with me. "Where's Aiden?" I asked.

Louis looked at me disgustingly. "Why would you care about that piece of garbage?" He turned around, avoiding the question.

Awkwardly, I followed Louis around to see his face. "What's wrong?" I asked concerned.

Louis stopped and laughed. "You know what's wrong..?" He looked me dead in the eyes. I could see that he had a couple scratches and a bruise. "That you like him." Louis stretched his arms so they would cover his face.

I tried to move Louis's hand away to examine how badly hurt he was but he wouldn't let me.

A couple seconds later, the gym door opened and a figure I haven't seen in a while appeared. Aiden.

Aiden walked towards us. He looked different than normal. His face was bruised a little and his lip was scabbed.

When Aiden stood in front of me, I reached up and touched his face. "Oh my gosh! What happened!" I frantically asked examining him. I twirled around him, looking for more bruises.

"He happened." Aiden pointed to Louis and shakes his head.

Louis scoffed. "He happened." Louis mocked. "You happened." Louis shoves Aiden.

Aiden pushes back Louis and they scowled at each other.

"You're a joke!" Louis yelled. "You don't deserve him!" Louis gets up in Aidens face.

I stepped in between the two and attempted to push them away.

Aiden retaliated and they began to throw insults at each other. Each getting worse and worse.

A clump of people across the gym watched them fight, whispering and making bets on who would win.

"Oh my gosh.." I started panicking. I never had to stop a fight, I was always the one in the fight! Typically, on the floor, getting kicked. All of a sudden, I felt overwhelmed and I started to breath heavily.

Louis and Aiden kept fighting and my head started to spin and I' was getting woozy. My knees buckled and I fell over onto the ground.

Aiden was the first to notice. He shoved his brother really hard and Louis fell on the floor. Seconds later, Aiden was by my side.

"Ethan! Are you okay?!" He frantically yelled, trying to get me to respond. Aiden was feeling my forehead and moving my face around, seeing if I was still alive. I laid on the ground, paralyzed, my eyes getting heavy.

Later that day, I found myself in a room I sorta recognized. I rubbed my eyes and tried to focus on something in the room. The spinning subsided. I looked around at my surroundings only to find that I was in the school nurses office. Oh, the memories. I chuckled, I should make a scrapbook.

"Hey." I heard a voice from across the room.

"Hello?" I whispered back, my voice was rough.

"How you feeling?" A familiar body walked up next to me. It put its hand on my forehead, feeling the temperature temperature. I recognized the hand, It was Louis.

"Just peachy." I smiled sarcastically and scooted up into a sitting position. "Where's Aiden?" I said looking around the room.

"Detention." Louis smirked.

I gave a concerning look. "Detention?" Louis didn't like my response at all. He frowned. "Why is he there?" I asked.

"Why do you have to like him?" Louis sneered. "He's a horrible person, he used to beat you up!" Louis began to yell. "He's no good for you!" Louis reached for my arm. "Can't you not like him?" He begged, shaking my arm.

"Louis..." I tried to make him stop.

"Look what he did to you!" Louis points at a couple scars, that I've failed to hide. "Look at what he did to me!" He points to his face, where there were a couple bruises and a couple fresh cuts.

"Stop.." I whined, taking his arm off me. "I'm not in the mood to talk about this!"

"You're not safe when you're with him!" Louis commanded.

My head snapped at him. "Stop saying such horrible things!" I yell back at Louis. "You're his brother!"

"What! Now, you're siding with him?!" Louis was frustrated.

"Stop talking!" Louis looks at me in disbelief.

"I give up!" Louis dramatically throws his hands up in the air and sighs. "If you get hurt, I warned you." Louis got up from the chair and headed towards the door. Once, he reached the door, he turned to me and sighed. "You'll regret it."

I huffed. "Who is he to tell me that I'll regret it! It's my decision! Not his!" I laughed. "You'll regret it." I mocked his voice and crossed my arms. Ugh! I'm so mad!

Hey guys! Sorry It took me so long to update, I've been super lazy.. I have no excuses... I hope you will enjoy the new chapter and will continue to read and support my stories! Don't worry, I'll continue to write this story! (Along with the other ones too) Hehehe~

Side note/ Please follow me on twitter @WattpadNamedL and tweet "I nominate Bully & His Crush #MyWattysChoice #Wattys2016 (I'm hoping more people will read my story and maybe I'll win a Watty Award, Or not XD)

A: If you could travel anywhere in the world, or universe, where would it be?

Q: I would like to travel to Seoul, South Korea and Tokyo, Japan! I also want to go to Bora Bora!

Chapter 26 - "I love you."

- -

It's Monday morning and I've been dying to see Louis. I haven't seen him since our fight. Was it a fight? It was more of him telling me to stay away from Aiden... I sighed. Whatever, It's not like Louis can avoid me forever. He's my best friend. At least, I still hope we are. We've never been this long with out each other.

I glanced around the halls, searching for him. No signs. I headed to my gym class. I know I could see him there. He was always there before everyone else. He liked to be extra early so no one could see him change.

I walked through the locker room door and headed over to his locker. I looked around and sighed in relief when I saw him changing. Finally, I can talk to him. I jogged towards him and stopped abruptly in front of him.

"Louis-" I yelled but he cut me off by slamming the locker door. Woah.

I lightly grab his arm, "Louis!" I shouted again. He pushed my hand off him. Someone was angry.

Louis turned his head and looked right at me, frustrated. "I've had enough." He says quietly.

I scoffed. "Seriously? That's the first thing you say to me?" I grab his arm again, this time more forcefully. "Louis!"

Louis tore my wrist off his arm and holds it up in the air, like some trophy. I struggled to break through his grasp. I knew he was strong but I didn't think he was this strong.

Louis reached for my other arm and used all his strength and shoved me into the locker wall. Trapping me with his frame. My wrists were by my head.

"ETHAN!" He yells. "WHY CANT YOU-" he stops and releases his hands that were trapping me. Louis turns his head and avoids eye-contact.

"STOP IGNORING ME." I shouted. I grabbed his shirt into fists. "Look at me!"

I could tell that Louis looked like he was about to cry. "I can't take it anymore!" He shouted.

"Can't take what anymore?!" I cried back. "I miss my best friend!" I pulled his shirt closer to me. Louis was two inches away from me. I could feel the body heat between us. There was an enormous amount of tension between us.

Louis puts both his hands on each side of my neck and lifts my head up a little bit with his thumbs. He moved his face closer to mine, I could feel his breath on my cheeks. He leaned in a couple inches closer and his lips touched mine. A tear left his eye.

I didn't move, I couldn't. My brain stopped working, I don't know what I felt. I just stood there for what seemed like eternity. I could feel all of Louis's emotions with just one single touch.

Louis released my neck and dropped his hands to his side. He looked at me, crying. Whispering. "I'm sorry." Another tear left his eye. "I love you." Louis backs up, leaving a space in between us. I could feel the cold wind drift between us.

After a second of utter silence, I raised my arm and brought it to his cheek. I felt how warm it was. Louis turned his head into my hand. I could feel how much he longed for me. I released my hand and brought it out a couple inches. Next thing I know, I slapped him. Really hard.

I can see Louis's cheek turn blushed cheek turn bright red. He looked at me, confused, as if why I did that. I opened my mouth but nothing came out. No words, no sounds, nothing but air. I stood back and watched him try to comfort his pain.

I turned away and headed towards my locker. I slammed it open and threw my shirt off. There was a mirror next to my locker and I glanced myself in it. My face was flushed, and there was some bruising on my wrists. I turned back to my locker and stood there. Trying to connect everything that happened.

I put my gym shirt on and turned around. Louis was watching me. Without thinking I said the first thing that flew out of my head. "WHY!" I began yelling at Louis. "WHY DID YOU DO THAT?" The emotions were just flying out of me. I couldn't stop them.

Kids were entering the room. I ran over to Louis and pushed him down on the ground. "YOU!" I grabbed his shirt and bunched it up, making his face closer to mine. "HOW COULD YOU DO THAT TO ME?" I screamed in his face. I reclined my arm and punched him in his face. I began crying. "YOU WERE MY BEST FRIEND!" I punched him again.

Kids were surrounding us in a circle, watching me beat up Louis, yelling "Fight! Fight!" I punched Louis again and again. Mumbling, "Why... Why did you do that..." Louis didn't fight back, he just took every single punch I gave him.

The teacher walked in the room and rushed over to push me off Louis. I fell onto the ground but tried to get up. The teacher was yelling at us to break it up. A couple of my classmates were trying to hold me back. I launched myself at Louis, getting one last punch in. I could hear Louis yelling "I'm sorry!" over and over.

Hey guys! I know it's been a while since I updated, my computer broke so I had to get a new one. Anyways, I hope this chapter was a good one and that I made it up to you for not updating sooner.

Q: Are you a morning or night person?

A: Night.

I didn't mean to ruin your ships!! ;_; I also didn't mean to make it so dramatic!

Chapter 27 - He's mine | You picked me.

I was furious, but why? My best friend kisses me and I beat him up and he didn't even fight me back. He just took it. That's what upset me.

The teacher sent me to the office and I got suspended for a couple days. Honestly, that was what I needed. I didn't want to see him. I can't believe he did that. I was picking at my nails when something clicked. He warned me. Oh god! What do I do about Aiden? What do I tell him? Do I even tell him that his brother, my best friend kissed me?! I paced around my kitchen, searching for an answer.

I gave up and went back upstairs to my bed. I didn't want to deal with the rath of Aiden. I entered my room and sat down on my bed. Then it hit me, what is going to happen to Louis? Aiden wouldn't hurt me as bad as he would to his own brother...right?

I contemplated my choices. Leave it alone and protect myself or run over to their house and see if Louis is still alive. I scratched my head, vigorously and mumbled "What to do.. What to do..." over and over in a circle. That's it, I decided. I stood straight up and ran down the stairs.

When I reached their house and ran up to the doorbell. I pressed the button at least a thousand times. A minute passed by, I was getting anxious. Is he okay..? I knocked on the door until my knuckles were red. When suddenly, the door opened and I saw a familiar body in my way.

"HELLO?" Aiden looked at me crazed and out of breath. "WHAT? What are you doing here!?" He questioned. It looked as if he ran down the stairs. I analyzed the situation and entered his house without permission.

I could smell the food they were cooking and stormed through the kitchen, looking all over. I couldn't find him anywhere. Then the living room, the TV was on but no Louis. "Where is he?" I asked frantically. Without Aiden answering, I ran upstairs. Out of breath, I shoved Louis's bedroom door open. I exhaled in relief. "Thank god your okay!" I fell onto my knees, catching my breath.

Louis was sitting on his computer chair, he turned around and looked at me, bug-eyed. "What-" he stuttered. "What are you doing here?" he asked timidly. He got up from his chair and walked towards me. He stopped right in front of me and smiled.

"I thought-" I gasped for a breath. "He might have killed you!" I stood up and examined Louis. I touched his arms, lifting them up and down, making sure they still worked. "I'm sorry for punching you." I said while examining him. I touched his chest. "I was just mad at you." I looked up at him. Louis grabbed my wrists and smiled, sweetly.

"It's okay." He wrapped his arms around me, giving me a hug. I snuggled into him. "I was really worried that he might have hurt you."

Louis sighed and mumbled under his breath. "This again." Louis hugged me tighter.

We hugged it out for a little bit but then I heard a cough. "What do we have here?" The hairs on the back of my neck were standing straight up and I got goosebumps. I forgot about him for just a second and I already can feel the anger seeping off him.

I pushed Louis off me and backed away slowly. I turned around to see Aiden leaning against the door wall. His arms were crossed and he looked very frusterated. He stood up and walked towards Louis. "How many times..." He clicked his tongue. "Do I have to tell you.." Aiden walked behind me and wrapped his arms around my torso. "He's mine." Aidens face deadpanned.

Louis seethed with anger. His fists balled up. "He's not yours!" he yelled. "He's mine!" Louis walked towards us and snatched Aidens arms off me. "He's been mine for years!" I was in the middle of this, literally. This felt awfully familiar.

I spread my arms, trying to break up the fight. "I AM NO ONES!" I yelled. I pointed my fingers at Louis. "I am not yours!" I grabbed Aidens arms that snaked up my body and tore them off. I turned around. "I'm not yours!" I grabbed Aiden by the collar of his shirt and dragged him out of the room. I turned around and yelled at Louis, "You! Stay there!" I slammed the door to Louis's room.

Crap. What did I do? Why did I drag Aiden out by his shirt? I turned around and saw Aiden smirking. I let go of his collar. He started chuckling. "What?" I asked him.

"Nothing.." He smiled harder this time. I grabbed him by the collar this time. "What!" I demanded.

Aiden giggled. "You picked me." I let go of him.

I was confused. "What?"

"If you picked him, you wouldn't have dragged me out. You would have stayed in there with him and shoved me out." He smiled. "But you didn't." He said matter-of-factly. He smirked. "You picked me."

Aiden grabbed me by the waist and dragged me close to his body. I could feel his hot breath next to my ear. "You picked me." He kissed my neck. His grip tightened as I tried to escape. He snuggled me even closer, kissing my neck up and down. "Thank you." He whispered.

Chapter 28 - You win.

"**F**ine, you win." I pushed Aiden's muscular hands off me. "Go downstairs, I'll be down in a minute." I directed him down the hall, towards the stairs. Asking him to leave Louis and I alone.

I walked over to Louis's room and stood in front of his door. Aiden stared at me, like I was his prey heading towards my death.

Slightly frustrated, I sigh. "Just trust me, okay?" I politely knocked on Louis's door. Once, then twice. I backed away slightly, just in case.

"Go away!" Louis yelled through the door.

I grabbed the door knob and tried to twist it open. It was locked. I knocked on the door again. "Louis! Open the door!" I twisted the knob again, this time more frantically.

"NO!" Louis was determined to shut me out.

"If you don't open this door, I'll get Aiden to break it down!" I yelled back at him. I placed my hands on my hips, clearly frustrated.

That got him, I heard shuffling on the other side of the door, then a couple twists.

The door slammed open, revealing a red-faced Louis. "WHAT?" he cried in agony. "What do you want from me?"

Instant guilt filled my face. "I'm sorry.." I apologized. I shouldn't have bothered him..

I shoved my way past Louis and barged into his room, closing the door behind us. I didn't want Aiden to interrupt. I walked back to Louis and reached for his hand. I held it for a minute, locking our fingers together. "You know.." I say looking at his red eyes.

With my other hand, My fingers delicately traced the vein that traveled through his wrists up to his forearm, eventually reaching his shoulder. I squeezed it and continued up to his neck. I cupped his neck, gently brushing his ear. Louis leans into my hand. "You're mine." I say to him softly.

Louis looks at me, suddenly. I moved my hand up to his cheek, brushing away his tears. "You've always been mine." Momentarily, Louis stops crying and looks at me, and tilts his head with deep confusion and slight curiosity.

I trace Louis's lips, feeling every part. "It's just a different kind." I look up at him. Louis pushes his lips into my hands, kissing it ever so slightly. "You're mine." I smile sweetly, Louis smiles, showing his teeth. "Just not mine."

Louis stopped smiling, he kissed my hand again, and began to back away. He placed his hand on my face and gently felt every crevace. His fingers traced over my lips and over my cheeks, near my ears and down my neck.

"I'm sorry." I say. Louis shushed me, as if he was savoring this moment. "I want to be with you, just not the same way." I took a step backwards, hitting the door. "I'm so sorry." I tried to smile but couldn't. Tears fell down my face. I looked downwards, scared to face Louis.

I could hear Louis's footsteps get closer to me. I looked up slightly to see a raised arm coming directly at me. I flinched, scared he was going to hit me. Louis placed his hand on my shoulder instead, as if he was comforting me. "It's okay." He croaked out. "I knew it was never going to work.." He choked and squeezed my shoulder hard, letting me feel some of his pain. He rubbed my shoulder for a couple seconds and let go. "I'm going to need some time." He sucks in a breath of air, lifting his head, trying to hold onto his shattered pride. Louis tried to smile. "I'm okay. I'll be okay." He let go of my shoulder and backed away. He walked over to his desk, and stood there. He smiled at me, but tears were falling down his cheeks.

I turned around and shut the door, slowly, leaving Louis alone in his room. I slid down onto the floor, hugging my knees.

After a couple minutes of silent thinking, I slowly got up and walked down the stairs. I got about half way and saw that Aiden was pacing up and down, bitting his nails. He was mumbling something over and over. I stood there, watching him for a bit. I never really noticed how tall he was. He took long strides as he paced around. I was admiring his body when finally, he looked around and saw me.

Aiden had a surprised face as he rushed over to me and climbed up the stairs. He lifts my arms up, examining my body. He spun me around, "Are you okay?" He asks, worried. He keeps scanning me, looking for something wrong. "Did he hurt you?"

I grabbed Aiden's shoulders and tried to hold him in place. He squirmed around for a bit. "I'm fine."I said, he stopped moving and looked at me. I looked straight into his eyes and said "I'm okay." I attempted my best reassuring smile. Aiden wasn't fully buying it but he accepted my answer.

Aiden moved out of the way, grabbing my hand, we headed down the stairs. He walks over to the couch and sits down. He pats the seat next to his, signaling me to sit next to him. I sigh but gradually sit down next to him. Aiden moves his thumb in a soothing motion over my hand. It was really calming me down. "Thank you." Aiden voiced. He moves closer to my body. He turns his head, to look at me. He looks into my eyes, "I really do like you." He says. He wraps his arms around my body, hugging me tightly. He slightly kiss my neck, "I love you." He whispers in my ear.

I feel butterflies in my stomach, "Me too." I whisper back. Aiden jerks back and questions my existence, "You what?" He asks. I smile, playfully and look at his lips. I look up at his eyes, and then back down at his lips again. "I love you."

Aiden got so close, that we kissed, over and over.

Chapter 29 - Naughty Things (END)

It's been about a week since we've officially started to go out and honestly not much has changed. Louis is still in his 'not talking to me' and 'I'm clearing up my feelings for you' mode. So, I have no one to really talk about stuff too. I can't really talk to Aiden about how I'm feeling because well, he's my boyfriend. My heart skipped a beat and I laughed out loud for a second. Boyfriend.

I stopped at my locker and unloaded my books from my bag. I put a picture of Aiden in the back of my locker, so I can see him every hour. I grab the last notebook and stuff it in the back. I quickly shut the door and look around. I see Aiden hanging out with his friends at the other side of the room. I stand, quietly, and watch him. I studied the way he looked, the way he laughed with his friends, the way he placed his hand on another guys arm. Pang. I frowned, what is this feeling?

Our eyes locked and smiled greatly. His smile cleared any harsh feelings I had away. He waved slightly, acknowledging my presence. I let out a breath I was unknowingly holding. I smiled and waved back. Aiden walked over to me; excusing his friends.

"Hey." He swiftly says, batting an eye.

I chuckle, "Hey." I look around and take a step closer, and hold one of his hands. Our bags are hiding them. Aiden instantly smiles.

"Let's go on a date." He says quietly, so only I could hear.

My heart skips a beat and I nod my head with great acceptance.

"Friday. I'll pick you up." Aiden says.

Friday appeared a lot faster than I expected. I guess I was just super busy with the week. I picked out a super simple outfit. I didn't know what we were doing so I didn't want to dress to fancy or too casual. I picked out a simple black long-sleeve shirt and some nice dark jeans. Of course, I picked out a nice pair of sneakers. I styled my hair slightly different, making it spike up just slightly. I felt that give me a 'badboy esk' feel to it.

I heard the doorbell ring downstairs and rush down to answer it. I knew who it was going to be. Aiden, he looked magnificent. Really beautiful. He wore a button down shirt with his normal biker jacket and some nice jeans. I sighed in relief, I picked the right thing to wear.

He smiled at me, eyeing my up and down. Checking me out as I checked him out. He is some eye-candy. Aiden grabbed my hand and squeezed tight. "You look hot." He choked out.

I laughed. "So, do you!" We both joked.

He led me to his car and opened the door for me. I hopped in and situated myself. I grabbed the seat belt and tried to buckle but it wasn't budging. Aiden hopped back in his car and looked over at me. He sighed. "What am I going to do with you?" He leaned over to me, our faces close together. Eyes locked. Click, the buckle fastened. Aiden smiles, all toothy. "I bet you wanted me to kiss you." He backs away from me and fastens his own. I pouted. He was right.

Aiden reverses the car and heads down the road. He stops at a stop sign. He quickly leans over to me and kisses my cheek. He rushes back to normal position and presses the gas petal. "I can't leave you hanging." I smiled and giggled, trying not to let him know that I enjoyed it.

Neon lights flashed around and I could see that we were at the bowling alley. I looked at Aiden. He sheepishly smiled. "I didn't want to be stereotypical." He unbuckled his seat and opened his door. He walked over to my side and opened the door for me. If the night keeps going like it's been, it was going to be a great night.

We enter the alley and walk up to the counter. Aiden pays for our tickets and the man asks for our shoe sizes. Once we exchange shoes, we walk over to our lane. I pick up a bowling ball and realize that I'm weak! I couldn't pick up the ball! I casually walked away from the ball and picked a different one that seemed lighter. Still too heavy, I tried once again, and finally, it was good.

I threw the ball down the lane and it ended up in the gutter! I sighed. Aiden picked up his and threw it down the aisle too. Luckily for him, it ended up being a strike! "WOW!" I cheered for him. "You wanted to show off, didn't you!" I groaned at him. Aiden smirked.

"Come on, I'll show you how to do it." He walks over to me and hands my ball to me. I stand up and aim. Aiden reaches over me and grabs my arm. He aims for me. Our bodies our touching and I can feel the heat radiating off him. I reacted so strongly to his touch, I jerked up and the ball went flying in the other lane. My face turned bright red.

"Well, that's one way to do it." He laughed, holding his stomach.

I tried a couple more times and improved a little bit. By the end of the game, we we're getting hungry. We ended up leaving the alley and ended up at a nearby ice cream shop.

I ordered a strawberry cone and Aiden ordered a banana split. We sat down at a table that was out of the way of others. I grabbed Aiden's spoon and tried some of his ice cream. "MMM..." I slurped down the ice cream. "That was good!" I say, taking another bite of his. He smiles, "You should gotten this one then!" He steals back his spoon and eats a bite. We chuckle.

"Let me try yours!" I hold the strawberry cone out, in front of his mouth. Aiden sticks out his tongue and licks it very slowly. He looks me in the eyes, making the whole experience very sensual. He licks his lips, enjoying the strawberry ice cream. He takes another lick, this time extra slow and turning around the cone. Making sure to get all the sides. His eyes change to a darker color.

I suck my breath in, taking in what Aiden's doing to me. I could feel myself getting bothered.

Aiden, licks his lips, making sure to get all the spillage. He bites his lip and looks at me, even deeper. "Oh, the things I could do to you." He smirks and sits back. Watching me, flustered. I cough, trying to clear the air but it's not working very well. I can feel the hairs on the back of my neck stand straight up.

"I'm going to get some fresh air." I rise from the chair and walk outside. I walk around the building, my hand grazing the wall. I yell, from frustration. I lean against the wall, catching my breath and trying to calm down my nether region.

A couple minutes passed by and I was ready to go back in, but before I could even get off the wall, there was a mysterious body against me. I looked up, trying to identify who it was. Luckily, it was Aiden.

Aiden used one of his hands to pin my hands above my head. I groaned, as he moved me. With the other hand, he cupped my waist. His hand slipped under my shirt. His hands were cold, from the ice cream. It made me shiver and let out a weird sound. He raised his hand up and everything was sticking straight up. Everything. "Aiden." I pleaded with him.

He smushed his body onto mine, His equally, hard. "Every time, I see you." Aiden kissed my neck. "You make want to do things to you." He sucked and left a visible mark. He licked my ear. "Naughty, things." He turned and faced me. Our eyes, locked. He leaned in closer, and kissed my lips. At first, it was nice and sweet but then got darker and heavier.

It continued that way until we couldn't handle it anymore. Our clothes were shifted and our hair messy. Aiden looked at me and kissed my forehead. He kissed my eyelids, my nose bridge, my cheeks and finally my lips. "I love you so much." He kisses my lips, once more.

"So do I." I kiss him back and hug him tightly. "So do I." I repeated.